# NORMAN BRIDWELL

# Clifford's®
## FIRST SNOW DAY

## SCHOLASTIC INC.
New York   Toronto   London   Auckland   Sydney

For Emma and Jake

The author thanks Manny Campana
for his contribution to this book.

ISBN 0-590-03480-4

Copyright © 1998 by Norman Bridwell.
All rights reserved. Published by Scholastic Inc.
CLIFFORD and CLIFFORD THE BIG RED DOG and associated logos are trademarks
and/or registered trademarks of Norman Bridwell.

15  16  17  18  19  20                                    01  02 03

Printed in the U.S.A.    24

First  printing, October 1998

I'm Emily Elizabeth,
and this is my dog, Clifford.
We love to play in the snow.

I remember the first time Clifford saw snow.
He was just a tiny puppy. It was his first winter.

Snow had been falling all night long.

In the morning, I got dressed to go outside.

I said, "Clifford, I have a surprise for you."

He was surprised.

Clifford had a little trouble walking in the snow.

Then he found a way to keep up with me.

We walked to the park.

The kids were going down the hill on their sleds.
I thought Clifford would enjoy a ride.

I forgot he couldn't hold on to the sled.

I had an idea.

Now Clifford could slide down the hill, too.

Afterward, we went over to the pond.
Skaters were whizzing by.

Before I knew it, Clifford ran onto the ice!

He spun around and around.
I was scared. I couldn't reach him.

Oh no!

I yelled, "Watch out for my puppy!"

That was close!
I had to get Clifford out of there fast.

"Help!" I called.

But could the boys hear me?

Hooray! My puppy was safe.

We thanked the hockey player for his good deed.
Then it was time to head back home.

On the way I saw my friend Tim.
He was making a big snowman.

He asked me to help him.
Tim made the bottom part...

...and I made the middle.

Then Tim rolled a smaller ball to make the snowman's head.

I put the snowman's middle in place,
and then I looked around for Clifford.

He was nowhere to be seen. Where did he go?

While Tim was putting a cap on the snowman,
I called and called for Clifford.

We heard a sound. "Hey, look!" Tim said.
"The snowman's nose is moving!"

It was Clifford!
Thank goodness I found him.

That was enough snow for one day.

We rushed home for some nice warm soup.

My puppy's first snow day was quite an adventure.

Snow days are even more fun now that Clifford has grown up.
What a wonderful dog.